onkers

First published in 2016 in Great Britain by
Barrington Stoke Ltd
18 Walker Street, Edinburgh, EH3 7LP

www.barringtonstoke.co.uk

Text © 2016 Tony Bradman
Illustrations © 2016 Tom Morgan-Jones

A CIP catalogue record for this book is available
from the British Library upon request

ISBN: 978-1-78112-503-8

Printed and bound by CPI Group (UK) Ltd, Croydon, CR0 4YY

Tony Bradman,
Master Scribbler

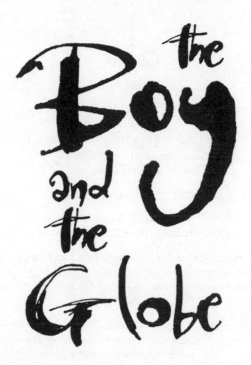

the Boy and the Globe

With inky daubs by Tom Morgan-Jones

Conkers

This one is for Hilary

THE
Cast

TOBY CUFFE . . . . an orphan boy

JACK FILCHER . . . . a young thief

WILLIAM SHAKESPEARE . . . . . a writer of plays

MOLL CUT-PURSE . . . . a trainer of young thieves

JOHN HEMINGES
HENRY CONDELL
AUGUSTINE PHILLIPS } . . . play-house people and
RICHARD BURBAGE   actors from The Globe
ROBERT ARMIN

NED ALLEYN . . . . an owner of a rival
play-house

SIR EDMUND TILNEY . . . . . . Master of the Revels to
King James

KING JAMES . . . . a monarch

SARAH . . . . a girl who Toby meets

A TAVERN KEEPER, VARIOUS ROUGH BOYS, GENTLEMEN,
PLAY-HOUSE AUDIENCES, OTHER RESIDENTS OF LONDON

THE
Place

London

THE
Time

The years 1611 and 1623

ACT I: The Story

ACT II: Funne Activities for Boyes & Girls

ACT I

The
Story

SCENE ONE

Queen of the Pick-Pockets

The inn stood on the corner of a narrow street just off Cheapside, the great road that led from St Paul's and into the heart of London. The sign over the door said The Devil's Tavern. This was the place Toby was looking for. He took a deep breath and went inside.

Beyond the door was a large, dark room full of people drinking and shouting and laughing raucously. Toby had been in taverns

before, so he knew what they were like, but
this one seemed especially rough. He looked
around at the people sitting at the tables, and
the few who were standing, but none of them
seemed to be the person Toby was after. He
went up to the bar. The tavern keeper had a
shiny bald head, a purple nose and a sagging

belly that arrived quite some time before the rest of him. He peered down at Toby.

"Begging your leave, sir," Toby said. "Where can I find ... you-know-who?"

"Another lamb for the slaughter, eh?" the tavern keeper snorted. "She's in the back room with her band of rogues." He nodded to a door in the corner.

Toby thanked him, opened the door he had indicated, and went into an even darker room. It was lit by a couple of smoky lanterns and Toby had to peer through the thick air to see who else was there. There were a dozen or so tough-looking boys leaning against the walls, but none took any notice of Toby, so he stood beside them. A small, skinny boy was standing alone in the middle of the room, and in front of him a figure sat on a big chair like a throne. Deep shadow covered the figure's face – then suddenly a powerful voice came out of the darkness.

"*Books?* What am I supposed to do with a few blasted *books*, you dolt?"

"Sorry, Moll!" the boy squeaked, clearly

terrified. "I just don't know what I was thinking, really I don't. I saw 'em lying there and I grabbed 'em and ran!"

The person sitting in the chair stood up into the light, and Toby saw it was a woman. She was tall and broad-shouldered and she wore a man's leather jerkin over a woman's raggedy gown. She had a tangle of black hair like the nest of an incredibly messy bird, and a face that looked as if it could turn you to stone. So this was Moll Cut-Purse, the Queen of London's thieves and pick-pockets.

"Don't do it again," Moll snarled at the boy. She grabbed a book from a table beside her chair and flicked through it. Then she threw it down again. "When I send you out to

5

do some thieving it's gold and silver I want, or at least something I can sell. Why, I'll wager the printers themselves couldn't even sell this lot. Not that we know what any of them are about, do we? Seeing as ... *NONE OF US CAN READ!*"

She shouted the last few words, and the boy winced as if she had struck him. The rest of Moll's boys laughed and jeered and called him nasty names. Toby had heard a lot of swearing on the streets of London, but some of their curses were new to him.

"Er ... perhaps I could help?" he said, stepping forward. "I can read."

"Is that right?" Moll said, glaring at him. "And who might you be?"

"Toby Cuffe at your service, my lady,"
Toby said, with a bow.

"Oooh, listen to him." Moll raised a
thick eyebrow and grinned. "He might look
like a common street-child and a beggar,
but he sounds like a
gentleman."

The band of
rogues began to
laugh at Toby now,
and called him nasty

names too. He glanced down at himself. True, his jacket and breeches and stockings were old and tatty and dirty, and his shoes were falling apart. He had found them on a rubbish tip, so there hadn't been much wear in them to begin with.

"Well, you're half right," he said. "I have been living on the streets, but I would rather die than be a beggar."

"Ah, I like a boy with a bit of ambition," said Moll, sitting down on her throne once more. "Well, let's hear your story, then, puttock. It had better be a good one, mind."

"There's not much of a

story to tell," Toby said, shrugging. "And I'm sure you'll have heard it before. There are plenty of orphans with a tale like mine ..."

But Moll waved her hand for him to go on and so he explained that he was born and bred in London, the son of a carpenter and a seamstress. Life had been good and they had been happy – until two years ago, when an outbreak of the Plague had changed everything. First it had killed his hard-working father, then his two pretty little sisters, and finally it had carried off his saintly mother. He had no other family, so he'd been fending for himself ever since.

"Stop, you're breaking my heart!" Moll wailed, wiping the tears from her cheeks with the sleeve of her dress. She blew her nose in it too, with a noise like a trumpet. "Those poor little girls!" she said. "They must have gone straight to Heaven to live with the angels."

"Er ... yes, I'm sure you're right," said Toby. "I hope so, anyway."

In fact, his "pretty little sisters" had never actually existed. He had invented them to make his story even sadder, and it seemed to have worked. His mother would have given him a clip round the ear for telling such an outrageous fib, and his father wouldn't have been too pleased, either. But his parents were gone, and Toby had learned the hard way that you had to do whatever it took to survive when you were on your own. Especially when the

people you were
dealing with were
this scary.

"So what
happened after that?"
Moll said. She leaned forward on
her throne, clearly eager to hear the rest of
Toby's story. "How have you been getting by?"

"Not very well," said Toby. "Oh, I've tried
to earn a living doing odd jobs, and I sleep
wherever I can find a place. But it hasn't
been easy, and I've been so cold and poor
and always hungry. I haven't eaten for three
days."

There was more to it than that, of
course. Toby had a dream that one day he

would live in a house again, with a family of his own, and be just as happy as before. But to make that dream come true he would have to start earning some proper money.

"And now you've come to me," Moll said, smiling. "Why would that be?"

"Because you teach boys to be thieves and pick-pockets," said Toby. He had tried to stay honest, but that was hard for a boy alone on London's streets. "And you take good care of all those who work for you. That's what I've heard, anyway."

"You heard right – didn't he, boys?" said Moll. There was a murmur of agreement from the band of rogues. "I know a good lad when I see one too, and I'd be glad to take you on. So long as you understand what you're letting yourself in for." She bent closer to Toby. "If you get caught stealing anything worth less than a shilling they'll chop off your right hand," she warned. "More than a shilling and they'll hang you. Still want to be one of us?"

"Better to be hanged than starve to death, I suppose," said Toby, although in truth he would rather have avoided both fates. But Moll just laughed, spat in her hand and held it out to him. Toby did the same, and they shook hands to seal the deal.

Moll sent him out thieving the very next day.

SCENE TWO

A Visit to the Play-House

Toby quickly took to his new life. It helped that he was getting regular meals for the first time in two years, and that he had a proper place to sleep, a corner of the back room in The Devil's Tavern. The thieving wasn't as difficult or scary as he had thought it would be, although he did sometimes think of his parents and feel a twinge of guilt. Moll sent him out with other boys, and to begin with he kept watch while they did the work. They were friendly and keen to help him learn their skills.

Some were *dippers* – that meant they could pick a rich man's pocket without him knowing. Then there were the *nippers*, boys who could snatch a gold necklace from a rich lady's throat and run away so fast they'd be streets away before she even knew it was missing. Last but not least were the *cut-purses*, the princes of the thieving world. They usually worked in pairs. One boy would distract the victim while the other cut the fat purse from his belt.

"Then I slip it to you," Jack Filcher told Toby. He was the small, skinny boy Moll had told off that first afternoon. "And you scarper

just as fast as you can. Got that?"

They were sitting in the back room of The Devil's Tavern with the others. It was morning, and they were having breakfast – bowls of porridge and mugs of small beer – while they waited for Moll to arrive and give them their orders for the day.

"Er ... yes, as fast as I can," Toby

muttered, although he was more interested in the book he was reading. Toby had read all the books Jack had stolen, but he kept returning to this one, *A Discovery of the Bermudas*. It was an amazing story of a sea voyage and a shipwreck on some distant islands, off the coast of America. Toby loved to read stories of gallant adventurers and exotic lands far, far away. He knew he wasn't the only one, either. Everybody was interested in such things these days.

"I see you've got your nose in a blasted book again, puttock!" Moll cuffed Toby good-naturedly on the ear. Toby jumped – he hadn't heard her come in. "Don't see the point of them myself," she added.

"They're a lot of fun," said Toby. "You find out all sorts of interesting stuff in them, too. That's why my mother made sure I was taught how to read."

"And *I'm* sure she's looking down from Heaven, pleased I'm taking care of you so well," said Moll, beaming at him. "I'm sending you to a play-house today."

Most people in London loved play-houses, special places where you could watch players acting out stories on a stage. Toby's parents had taken him a few times before they had died. But he had been too small to see much, and the crowd had been loud and smelly. Of course, he hadn't been back since. It cost a penny to stand in front of the stage, more if you wanted a seat, and Toby needed all the coins he ever had to put food in his belly.

The rest of the boys started clamouring round Moll, everybody wanting to be sent to a play-house. "*QUIET!*" Moll yelled eventually. "Don't be so daft, you can't *ALL* go – you would cause a riot. No, it will just be Toby and Jack."

"Which play-house are you sending us to, Moll?" Jack asked, his voice squeaky with excitement. "The Fortune? The Curtain? My favourite is The Red Bull ..."

"Actually, I'm sending you to The Globe," Moll said, and Jack frowned.

"What, south of the river?" he said. "It's a bit dodgy over there, isn't it?"

Moll laughed at the expression on his face. "Just the right place for a common thief like you then," she said. "Here's a penny each to get you in, and don't come back till you can make me a rich woman."

It was a sunny summer's day, and Jack and Toby chatted and laughed as they made their way through the packed London streets. Toby had known hard times in the city, but he still loved the place. It was always full of life and energy and people, good and bad. He loved the smells and the noise, the great cathedral of St Paul's with its spire reaching into the sky, the streets of shops and stalls selling pies and gloves and books and sweets and everything else you could possibly imagine. He loved the wide river, and the bridge that crossed it.

But like Jack, Toby wasn't quite so sure about Southwark, the area south of the river. People went to the part of Southwark called Bankside to spend their money on having fun, and it had a reputation for being a wild place. There were taverns where men got drunk and brawled with each other, and places where you could gamble on fights between bears and bulls and dogs. Until now, Toby had thought it best to stay well away.

Jack pushed through the crowds – Bankside was even busier than the City – and

Toby followed. They turned a corner, and Toby found himself looking up at a tall building with a thatched roof. It was clearly a play-house, but Jack kept walking. Toby stopped, confused, and called after him. "Hey, Jack! Isn't this the Globe?"

"No, that's The Rose," Jack said. "It's been empty for years, ever since the last owner went bust, I think. Mind you, I've heard a whisper it's going to be re-opened soon. Someone has certainly been doing a bit of work on it." Toby saw that Jack was right – some of the walls seemed to have been freshly painted.

A few moments later they turned a corner and arrived at The Globe.

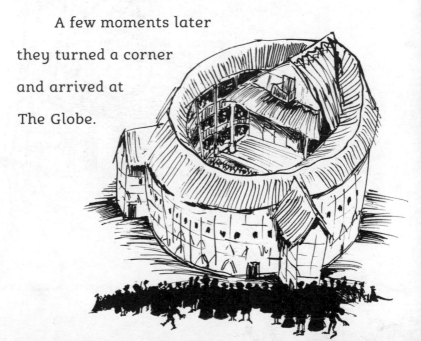

It was a similar building to The Rose, but
where The Rose was shut-up and quiet, this
was clearly a working play-house. The main
doors were open and a large, cheerful crowd
was pressing its way in, people calling out to
friends or pausing to buy food and drink on
their way in.

"Come on then, let's get to work," said Jack. "Remember, follow my lead."

They paid their pennies and went inside. Jack kept to the edge of the crowd, his eyes darting here or there as he looked for a suitable victim. Eventually he darted off, nodding at Toby to follow. But Toby was too busy looking at the stage with its painted pillars and curtained openings, and the galleries full of rich people looking down. Soon he heard strange music, and three players dressed as witches emerged onto the stage.

"*When shall we three meet again?*" one

said. "*In thunder, lightning, or in rain ...*"

It was a wonderful play, the story of a Scottish king called Macbeth. Toby was terrified by the witches and gripped by the twists and turns of the plot. He was tall enough now to see and hear everything, and he loved the whole experience. Being part of the audience was fun too – he groaned and gasped and yelled with everyone else. He had no idea the play-house could be so much fun.

After a while Jack appeared at his side. "Pssst! Toby!" he muttered. "Fat lot of use you've been, leaving me to get on with things by myself. Here, take this ..."

Jack pushed a fancy purse into Toby's hand, then vanished into the crowd. Toby

dimly remembered that he was supposed to do something, but the witches were on the stage again and he desperately needed to know what was going to happen next.

"*Double, double, toil and trouble,*" another one said. "*Fire burn and cauldron bubble ...*"

Suddenly rough hands grabbed Toby from behind, almost choking him.

"I've got the rascal!" somebody yelled. "Steal my purse, would you, worm?"

Toby had a feeling things had just taken a rather bad turn.

SCENE THREE

Not Good for Business

Toby struggled, but he couldn't escape. There were two men holding him, and they were very cross. One roughly snatched the purse from his hand, and then both of them did more yelling, as well as lots of cursing and swearing. Eventually the other people nearby started to yell at them. "Be quiet! We can't hear the play!" Then someone threatened to pour a mug of beer down on them from the gallery, and that finally made them pay attention.

The two men dragged Toby off to the side of the play-house and pushed him up against the wall. Toby could see them more clearly now. They were young gentlemen, both

dressed in fine silks and velvet, with pearls dangling from their ears and expensive swords on their belts. One of them whipped out a dagger and pressed it against Toby's throat. "I should slit your gizzard for daring to rob me," he snarled.

"Now then, friends," a calm voice behind them said. "We don't want any blood on the play-house floor, do we? It leaves a stain that's the very devil to get rid of."

The knife at Toby's throat was lowered and the two gentlemen stepped back, although they still held his arms tightly. Toby looked round them at the man who had spoken. He was tall and thin and had a kindly face, but a strong one too.

"Stay out of this," the gentleman with the dagger snarled. "This scurvy rascal had my purse in his hand, so I know he stole it. I will deal with him as I see fit."

The tall man's eyes locked onto Toby's. "Is this true, boy?" he said.

"No, sir, it most certainly isn't!" Toby said, thinking fast. "I didn't steal it, I, er ... came across it. I was going to find out who it belonged to so I could return it –"

"The knave is lying," the other gentleman said. "He's a common thief, and deserves to be hanged. And who are you to stick your nose in our affairs, anyway?"

"John Heminges at your service, gentlemen," the tall man said, bowing. "I am one of the sharers of The Globe play-house, so all that happens here matters to me ..."

Toby listened anxiously as the three men talked. The purse had been heavy with coins, so he realised his life really could be at stake. But for some reason Heminges seemed to be on his side, and was trying to calm the gentlemen down.

"There's no proof the boy stole your purse," he said. "And you have it again, so there's no harm done. Tell you what, let him go and I'll give you two free seats for tomorrow's show. We're doing *As You Like It*. Everybody loves a good comedy."

The gentlemen grumbled for a while, but they gave in at last and returned to watch

the play. Toby was about to thank his saviour
when Heminges grabbed him by his collar.
He dragged Toby outside and took him to the
rear of the building, then through a doorway.
They climbed a narrow staircase that led
up three flights to another door. Heminges
pushed it open without knocking.

"Can I leave you to deal with this lad,
Will?" he said. "I'm pretty sure he's a
nipper, or maybe a cut-purse.
I have to be back-stage for
the end of the show."

Heminges shoved Toby into the small room beyond the door. A large part of it was filled by a wide table beneath a window that looked down onto the play-house stage. A middle-aged, balding man was sitting at the table. He wore dark breeches and a white shirt stained with ink, and he had several books open in front of him and a quill pen in his hand. There was paper on the table too, all covered in spidery writing and crossings-out. The man sighed, and half-turned in his seat so that he was facing the door.

"I said I wasn't to be bothered, John," he groaned. "How can I be expected to write if you must always interrupt me? What am I supposed to do with him, anyway?"

"How should I know?" Heminges said. "You're the one with all the ideas."

"If only that were true," the man called Will murmured, putting a hand to his forehead.

Heminges laughed and turned to go, but Toby wanted to get something straight first. "Hang on," he said, addressing Heminges. "I don't understand – if you're so sure I *am* a pick-pocket, how come you saved me from those two downstairs?"

"Well, we can't have fine young gentlemen like them going around telling everyone they had their purses stolen at The Globe, can we?" said Heminges. "That wouldn't be good for business, and we've got enough trouble as it is."

"You can say that again," Will muttered, but Heminges had gone, leaving Will and Toby alone. Will looked at the papers in front of him, then back at Toby. "Listen, I really don't have time to deal with you at the moment," Will said. "I should be getting on with my work, not that I seem to be making much progress. Could you just sit quietly over there in the corner? At least until I've finished this scene."

Toby shrugged. "I'd be happy to," he said. Of course he knew he should probably try to get away – that's definitely what Jack or Moll would tell him to do. It would be easy, too. Will was distracted, scribbling and crossing things out and muttering to himself. But Toby didn't want to leave. He was intrigued by everything about the play-house. The play had been amazing, and now Toby saw that this room was like a paradise. There were lots more books in here, several shelves full of them, in fact.

Toby did his best to keep quiet and not disturb Will, but his mind was racing. "Can I ask you a question?" he said after a while, unable to stop himself.

Will heaved another sigh, and slowly turned to him. "If you must," he said.

"Have you read all these books? I've never seen so many in one room."

"Most of them," said Will, leafing through one on his desk. "I get ideas for my plays from them, even whole stories, sometimes ... Now can I get on with what I'm doing?"

"Oh yes, sorry, don't mind me," said Toby. "Although I wondered ..." Will heaved an even deeper sigh and stared at him. "What are you writing?" Toby finished.

"Mostly rubbish," Will said gloomily. He threw down his pen and leaned back in his chair. "I'm supposed to be coming up with another hit play, but I'm stuck."

"That sounds painful," Toby said, hoping the joke would cheer Will up, but Will didn't seem to get it. "So what happens if you can't get, well ... unstuck?" he asked.

"We could just keep putting on old plays, like *Macbeth*," Will said, nodding at the window. Toby could hear cheers and clapping coming from the play-house, so he knew the play was over. "But that's not going to work for ever. These days people want new stories all the time, plays that aren't anything like the ones they've seen before. That's hard to do, but if we can't give them what they want, they'll go elsewhere."

"Do you mean they'll go to another play-house?" said Toby. "Like The Rose?"

"Yes, I mean exactly that," said Will, giving him a puzzled look. "But why are you talking about The Rose? It hasn't been a working play-house for a long time."

"It will be soon, though," Toby said. "I've heard it's going to be re-opened."

"Really?" said Will, looking worried. "We'd better tell the others!"

He jumped up and left the room, dragging Toby with him.

SCENE FOUR

Under Pressure all the Time

The play-house was almost empty by the time Will and Toby arrived downstairs. Will led Toby up onto the stage and through one of the curtained doors into the space behind it, a large room packed with the players who had just performed *Macbeth*. It was strange for Toby to see them changing out of their costumes now, especially the witches, who turned out to have been played by boys not much older than him. Up close he could see how they'd painted their faces to make their cheeks look sunken and wizened, and how the long black wigs they wore made them look like women.

Will stepped up onto a bench and addressed everyone. "Another great show, lads, we'll all be rich and famous yet!" The players cheered, although some called out rude comments as well. "Now then, where are you, John?" Will called. Heminges was at the back of the room. He raised his hand and Will nodded. "Sharers' meeting in five minutes, all right?" Will said. "That means you too, Henry, Richard, Robert, Augustine …"

The sharers met in another part of the

play-house, in a room stacked with boxes full of interesting objects – old swords, crowns that were painted gold with glass jewels stuck on, even a skull that looked very real. Toby was beginning to see how the magic of the theatre was created.

A table was squeezed in among the boxes, and the six men sat round it. Toby stood behind Will. The men were all more or less the same age, and they all looked prosperous. 'There must be money in their business,' Toby thought.

"Out with it then, Will," Heminges said. "You're looking rather dismal."

"That's nothing new," one of the others quipped. "He always looks like that."

"Thanks, Henry," said Will. "I have a lot to make me feel dismal. And I've just heard some more bad news. Apparently someone plans to re-open The Rose."

There were several sharp intakes of breath, some head-shaking – and then a loud argument began.

At first Toby didn't understand any of it, but before long he had learned quite a lot about the world of the play-houses. It seemed they were in constant competition with each other, although The Globe had always done well. So well, in fact, that old Queen Elizabeth had allowed The Globe's players to be called The Queen's Men. Then she died and King James of Scotland inherited her throne, but he liked The Globe's players too, so now they were called The King's Men.

But they had no guarantee that The Globe would continue to be so successful. Running a play-house was clearly a tough business. And having to compete with another play-house that was very close by would only make it a lot harder.

There was paper on the table, pens and ink, and Toby noticed something written on a sheet in front of Will. Toby peered over his shoulder and saw that Will had doodled the men's full names in his spidery handwriting – John Heminges, Richard Burbage – he had played Macbeth, Toby realised! – Henry Condell, Robert Armin – who had been the porter in the play! – and Augustine Phillips. There were some notes too, and Will had done a doodle round his own full name – William Shakespeare.

"Right, hold on, everybody," Heminges said at last. "I think we might be getting ahead of ourselves here. This is only a rumour – from an unreliable source."

The men all turned to stare at Toby, clearly expecting him to say something.

"Er … I trust the person who told me," he said. It was the right thing to say, even if it wasn't really true. He liked Jack, and Moll too, but he didn't trust either of them. "And you've only got to look at The Rose to see that someone has done a bit of painting."

"The boy is right," Henry Condell said. "I wondered about that myself."

"Well, I say there's no point worrying about a storm till it starts raining," said Augustine Phillips. "Besides, we have our wonderful Will, so we'll be fine."

Now they turned to stare at Will, all of them smiling.

Will shook his head. "Oh no, I'm not having that," he said. "I've told you, I'm fed up with being the one everybody else depends on. None of you understand what that feels like. I've been churning out play after play for nearly twenty years now, while you lot just sit around waiting for me to produce yet another masterpiece. We're supposed to be sharers in the play-house, but nobody shares what *I* go through. I'm under pressure all the time, and I hate it."

During Will's rant Toby noticed Condell and Phillips looking at each other and rolling their eyes, as if they'd heard it all before. But Will didn't see them.

"Come on, Will," Heminges said with a sigh. "You know we've been trying to take the pressure off you. What about all those hot new writers we've got lined up? They come highly recommended, particularly John Fletcher and Thomas Middleton. You can think up the plots for them, then they'll do the hard work. You could even do a bit of the fancy writing, if you like – you've always enjoyed showing off."

"But that's not now, is it?" Will groaned. "I've still got to write a new play for this season. We've been struggling to fill the play-house, and we badly need a hit."

"And I'm still waiting for that brilliant part you promised me," Armin said sulkily. "I mean, the porter in *Macbeth* doesn't have a whole lot of great lines, does he?"

"You'd only mess them up if he did," Burbage muttered. "Anyway, Will needs to concentrate on writing something that's got a big, dramatic part for *me*."

Everybody started squabbling again – everybody, that is, except Will and Toby.

"*QUIET!*" yelled Will after a while, and the others fell silent once more. "You see what I mean?" Will said, turning to Toby. "Don't ever be a writer, boy."

Toby thought it was a strange thing to say. Couldn't Will see how amazing it was to have written a play like *Macbeth*? There had been something magical in the way it had enchanted everyone in the play-house. Maybe he needed someone to remind him of how lucky he was to be doing what he did, of how lucky they all were. After all, none of them looked as if they had to worry about where they'd get their next meal.

"So then, what are we going to do about The Rose?" Heminges said at last.

"We should ask around, try and find out who's backing it," said Condell.

"Good luck with that," said Will. "Anybody who knows anything will clam up as soon as we start asking questions, won't they? After all, we're the competition."

"Begging your pardon, sirs," Toby said. "I could try and find out more."

Everybody turned to stare at him again. "Could you now?" said Will, suddenly interested. He glanced at Heminges, who shrugged and nodded. One by one, the others murmured their agreement as well. "That might be very useful, er –" Will waved a hand in the air. "What did you say your name was, lad?"

"I didn't, sir, nobody asked me," said Toby. "I'm Toby Cuffe. And I'm afraid I'll have to charge you a fee for my services. Shall we say ... sixpence?"

Will smiled. "Sixpence it is," he said. "Although for such an enormous sum we'll want some excellent information. We need it as soon as possible, too."

"Don't worry, sir," said Toby, smiling back at him. "You can rely on me."

Moments later Toby was running through the streets of London, making for The Devil's Tavern. He only hoped Jack would be there when he arrived.

And that Moll wouldn't be angry with him for getting caught.

SCENE FIVE

A Jack of Many Trades

"Well then, what have you to say for yourself, young Master Cuffe, my puttock?" Moll snarled, holding him by the ear. "Jack tells me you were hopeless, and he saw you getting caught as well. You're not going to make me rich like that, are you?"

Moll had seized him as soon as he'd come through the door of the back room at The Devil's Tavern. All the other boys were

standing around laughing as he wriggled in her grip. All of them, that is, except Jack, who was looking worried.

"Oww! I'm really sorry, Moll," Toby said. "I'll do better, I promise I will."

"Just make sure you do," said Moll, letting him go at last. Then she stared at him with suspicion in her eyes. "Hang on, how did you get away?" she asked.

"I, er ... made a run for it when they weren't looking." Toby had thought it best to make his story simple and not tell Moll the truth of what had happened. Some things were better kept to yourself, especially where money was concerned.

"Is that so?" said Moll, looking him up and down. "Well, it seems you're not as useless as I thought. Maybe I should train you up as a nipper instead."

It was a while before Toby was able to get Jack on his own for a chat. They sat in the darkest corner of the back room while Jack slurped broth out of a wooden bowl. There was no dinner for Toby tonight, after he'd let Moll down.

"I was interested in what you were saying about The Rose," Toby whispered. "Er ... you don't happen to know any more, do you? Like who's behind the plan to open it again?"

"No," Jack mumbled, licking his spoon. "Some rich man, probably."

"I need to know his name," Toby said.

"Really?" Jack was giving him a puzzled look. "What the devil for?"

"I'll tell you, but it has to be just between us, right?" Jack nodded, and Toby explained what had happened to him at The Globe, and what his mission was now. "Will you help me?" he said at last. "I'll give you, er ... tuppence if you do."

"Two whole pennies?" Jack said, grinning. "That'll boost my travel fund."

"Beg pardon?" said Toby. It was his turn to look puzzled now. "What's that?"

"Well, I don't want to spend the rest of my life in London, do I?" said Jack. "I'd like to visit the places I keep hearing people talk about – America, the Indies, China. So I've been saving my pennies. When I've got enough I'll set out on a great voyage." He looked vaguely into the distance, a dreamy expression on his face.

"I'll have to teach you how to read," said Toby. "You'd really enjoy some of those books

you stole. But in the meantime – how do I find out who wants to re-open The Rose?"

"Well," Jack said. "I suppose we could always break in and have a look around."

Toby goggled at him. "You know how to break into houses as well, then?" he said.

"Course I do!" Jack said, laughing. "I am a Jack of many trades ..."

They went to The Rose early the next morning. Jack said it was the best time to go as there wouldn't be many people around on Bankside at that hour of the day. Most of the locals would have stayed up very late, and would probably still be in bed sleeping off their sore heads.

Getting in turned out to be easy. At the back of the building Jack found a window that didn't fit properly, and soon he had it open. Toby gave him a leg up, then Jack pulled Toby in behind him. They crept down a dark corridor, through a room full of chests and boxes, and finally came to a closed door. Jack listened at it for a moment, then smiled. He pulled it open with a flourish and stepped through. Toby followed him – onto the stage.

As with The Globe, The Rose's top gallery was roofed with thatch, but the main circular section of the building was open to the sky. Soft morning light poured down from above, revealing the interior in all its glory. The galleries had been freshly painted, the space in front of the stage had been swept and cleaned, and the stage itself had been completely re-built. The pillars on either side of the stage were covered in patterns of gold and red, and at the rear was a brightly coloured back-cloth showing a street scene. In front of it was a large wooden chest, the kind that was used to store costumes at The Globe.

"I think we can safely say The Rose is going to be re-opened," Jack said admiringly. "Someone has been working hard ... this makes The Globe seem like a dump."

Toby knew Jack was right. Even in the short time he had spent at The Globe, Toby had noticed that the play-house run by Mr Shakespeare and his friends was a bit battered and run-down, the paint scuffed and faded, the stage creaking under the actors' feet. But Toby felt oddly protective towards The Globe. There was something about it, a magical quality this fancier play-house could never hope to match, however bright the new paint.

Suddenly they heard voices and footsteps coming their way. "No time to get out," Jack hissed, his eyes wide. "We'll have to hide! It's every man for himself!"

He made a dash for the wooden chest, threw it open, dived in, and closed the lid on top of himself. The voices and footsteps were getting closer, and Toby looked round desperately for a hiding place of his own. With seconds to spare he slipped into the narrow space between the back-cloth and the wall behind it. He peeked out, and was just in time to see two men coming into the theatre and climbing the steps onto the stage.

One was tall and broad-shouldered, and about the same age as Will Shakespeare. He wore an expensive-looking jacket of red and gold velvet with slashed sleeves that showed a fine silk shirt underneath. He had a great mop of yellow hair, and a face that seemed very pleased with itself. The second man was much older, a real greybeard, and he was dressed all in black. But his clothes looked expensive too, and he carried a long staff with a silver top.

"Well then, Sir Edmund, what do you think?" the tall man said, and his voice boomed out to fill the whole play-house. "We've finished in here, and by the end of the week the outside will also be done. We're planning to open the Friday after that."

"Excellent, Mr Alleyn," the older man said, in a high, piping voice. "Your play-house is most excellent. But it's the quality of the plays that counts in the end, isn't it? King James has grown rather bored with those he has seen of late."

"No wonder!" said Mr Alleyn. "If you ask me, Will Shakespeare is definitely losing his touch. Oh, he's had a good run, but his day is over, and I've hired some of the finest and most talented young writers of our times – John Fletcher, Thomas Middleton ..."

In his hiding place, Toby's eyes grew
wide. Those were the writers Heminges had
talked about for The Globe!

"You'll need plenty of good acting talent
as well," Sir Edmund said.

"Oh, don't worry, all the best actors

will come flocking to me when they see how successful we are," said Mr Alleyn. "My aim, Sir Edmund, is to persuade His Majesty to make *my* company The King's Men, and knock Shakespeare off his perch."

"Well, we'll see," Sir Edmund said. "But I have to say I'm rather impressed by what you've told me. Now, I have to get back to the Palace and report to the King."

Toby couldn't wait for them to go – he had a report of his own to make.

SCENE SIX

Let Slip the Dogs of War

"It's a disaster ... a total, utter, absolute disaster," Will said gloomily, shaking his head. "Or maybe it's a catastrophe ... Actually, it's a disaster *AND* a catastrophe!"

"Calm down, Will," said Heminges. "You're being a bit dramatic, aren't you?"

They were sitting round the same table at The Globe as before, along with the

other men – Condell, Phillips, Burbage and
Armin. Toby had just made his report to Will,
and was standing behind him. Jack was beside
Toby, looking very dapper in a fancy, puffed-

sleeve jacket that he had
"found" in the chest at
The Rose. He had wanted
to take some shoes as
well, but Toby hadn't given him time to try
them on.

"Being dramatic is what I do for a living,"
Will said. "Although if Ned Alleyn gets what
he wants, none of us will be making much of a
living in the future."

Will had instantly recognised the names
of the men Toby had overheard speaking
in The Rose. It seemed Ned Alleyn was an
old rival, a man who had started off as an
actor, but then had run play-houses all over
London – and made a lot of money out of them.

Sir Edmund Tilney was Master of the King's Revels. It was his job to keep an eye on the play-houses, and to seek out plays the King would like.

"I don't know what you're worried about, Will," Phillips said. "You always complain about writing, but you always come up with a new hit for us."

"Maybe I won't this time," said Will. "But even if I do finish the new play soon – and I'm pretty sure that I won't – we couldn't possibly get it on before The Rose re-opens. We need at least a couple of weeks for rehearsal. And if the King does drop us and makes Alleyn's company The King's Men, we might as well give up. We'll be finished – nobody will want to come to The Globe any more."

"Couldn't you just write a bit faster, Will?" said Condell. "That would help."

"Now why didn't I think of that?" Will laughed a wild laugh. Then he glared at Condell. *"THAT'S THE MOST STUPID THING I HAVE EVER HEARD!"* he roared.

Another loud argument broke out. Toby listened to the men yelling at each other, wishing he could help in some way. From what Will had said, it seemed all they really needed was a little more time so he could finish his new play. Then Toby remembered something Moll had said, and he had an idea.

"Begging your leave, gentlemen?" he said, raising his voice to be heard. The men fell silent and turned to look at him. "I was thinking, what if you could spoil things at The Rose? I mean, people wouldn't go there if it had a bad reputation – if, say, it was known as a place where you were bound to have your purse stolen."

"That's how it is in most play-houses anyway, as we know," Heminges said, giving Toby a look. "We're tough on it here, but people mostly take it for granted."

Toby blushed. "I'm sure you're right," he said. "Although I don't think there are many thieves and cut-purses in a play-house at any one time. Am I right, Jack?"

"You most certainly are, Toby," Jack said. "Too many thieves lead to trouble."

"Exactly," said Toby. "Imagine what it would be like if there were *dozens* of thieves and pick-pockets and cut-purses in The Rose for *every* play. It might start a riot."

"It might very well," Will murmured. "And is this something you can arrange?"

"Maybe," Toby said, shrugging. "I know the right person to talk to, at any rate."

"Interesting," said Will, and the others looked at each other, eyebrows raised. "But

of course, such a tactic would be very unfair,"
Will went on. "Some people might even say it
would be wrong, and a terrible sin to inflict
it on our fellow players." The others looked
sheepish. "Perhaps we should vote on it," Will
said. "Hands up all those in favour of knocking
Ned Alleyn down a peg or two in such a wicked
way?"

Each man raised his hand.

Will grinned, and turned to Toby. "Lead
on, young man!" he said.

So Toby and Jack took Will off to meet
Moll in the back room of The Devil's Tavern.
Toby was a trifle worried about bringing
the two of them together – they seemed to
come from such different worlds. But, in fact,

the Queen of Pick-Pockets and London's leading playwright got on very well right from the start.

"I've a feeling we might have a lot in common, Master Shakespeare," Moll said. "My boys are good boys, but they can be little rascals as well. Just like your actors and the others at your play-house. Tell me, how do you split the money?"

"Any profit we make is shared evenly between half a dozen of us," Will said. "We're the ones who put our money into the company in the first place. We pay everyone else according to the work they do."

Toby thought that seemed like a good way to arrange things, and Moll nodded too. "That's how I run my business too," she said, grinning. "Although I'm the only sharer."

Will chuckled.

"Now, about this job you want doing,"

Moll said. "You realise I'll have to charge you for it?"

"I wouldn't have expected anything else," said Will. "Name your price."

Moll came up with a figure that seemed enormous, but Will didn't bat an eyelid. Toby listened fascinated as they haggled, a lengthy process they both seemed to enjoy. At last they came to an agreement, and shook hands on the deal. Moll spat on hers first, of course, to make it official.

"*Cry havoc, and let slip the dogs of war!*" Will said.

Moll gave him a blank look.

"Sorry, it's a line from one of my plays," he said. "I just thought it fitted the occasion."

"I'm sure you did," Moll said. She patted his arm, then rolled her eyes at Toby.

Over the next few days playbills began to appear on walls all over London.

Grand Re-Opening of The Rose Play-House!
Under New Management!
Wonderful New Plays By New Writers!
Special Early Bird Deals!
Great Rates For Galleries!

There was a buzz of excited talk in the city about the re-opening, and on the big night The Rose was full to bursting. Ned Alleyn went onstage before the play began to address the crowds. "Welcome to The Rose!" he boomed. "This is a day none of us will ever forget ..."

He was right, but not for the reasons he imagined. The play started well enough – it was a comedy called *The Roaring Girl*, written by a pair of new playwrights, Thomas Middleton and Thomas Dekker. Toby was there, and he found himself quite gripped. But Moll had flooded The Rose with her boys, and before long people in every part of the play-house were yelling that they had been robbed. The audience stopped watching the play, and eventually there was a huge riot that spilled

out onto the streets.

The same thing happened at the next

show, and the next, and the one after that.

Sir Edmund ordered The Rose to be closed to prevent any more riots, although he hardly need have bothered. By then the actors were playing to an almost empty theatre.

"Job done, I think," said Will when he heard the news. Toby was with him, watching the players rehearsing on the stage of The Globe. "And it's all thanks to you, young Master Cuffe," Will added with a smile. "How can I ever –"

"WILL SHAKESPEARE!" somebody yelled. "I WANT A WORD WITH YOU!"

Toby looked round, and gulped.

Ned Alleyn was bearing down on them.

SCENE SEVEN

A Tale Told by an Idiot

Toby could see that Ned Alleyn had been a pretty good actor at one time. He had a *very* loud voice, and his anger seemed to fill the play-house like a great swirling storm. He ranted and raved, swearing at Will and calling him a whole string of nasty names that Toby had never heard before, not even from Moll's boys.

"It didn't take long to find out how you did it," Alleyn snarled at last. "You should be ashamed of yourself – using common thieves to bring down an old friend –"

"Old friend?" Will said with a snort. "Old enemy, more like. Don't try to deny that you planned to destroy The Globe. All's fair in love and war, Ned, and this is war."

"So be it," said Alleyn. "But you haven't beaten me. I haven't even started yet ... I'll soon talk old Sir Edmund round, and we'll be sure to keep out the cut-purses in future. You don't have a hope of winning in the long run."

"Oh, and what makes you so sure of that?" asked Will, smiling at him.

Alleyn moved closer, until his face was only inches from Will's. "It's simple, Will," he said. "Everybody knows you're struggling to come up with a hit. What's this you're rehearsing? *Hamlet*? I never thought that was much good when you put it on the first time. You'll be finished if you don't come up with something new."

Will didn't answer, but his smile faded, and Toby saw that he seemed to shrink into himself. Heminges was on the stage with the players, and now he jumped down and strode up to Alleyn. "Clear off, Alleyn!" he shouted. "You're not welcome here."

"And you won't be welcome anywhere when your pathetic excuse for a play-house finally goes bust." Alleyn laughed. "You'll all end up as beggars."

Then Alleyn stormed out. Heminges squeezed Will's shoulder. "Take no notice, Will," he said. But Will shrugged, and walked out himself.

Toby followed, expecting Will to go up to his room on the third floor of the play-house.

But Will headed in the opposite direction,
leaving the play-house and walking along
Bankside. There were few people around. Dark
clouds filled the sky, and a cold wind ruffled
the surface of the river. Will came at last to
St Saviour's, the big church that stood at the
southern end of London Bridge, and he
went into the graveyard. He sat

down on an ancient stone bench behind the church, and after a moment Toby sat down beside him.

Will was gloomily muttering to himself. "*Life's but a walking shadow, a poor player that struts and frets his hour upon the stage, and then is heard no more.*" He sighed and sank his head into his hands, then went on. "*It is a tale told by an idiot, full of sound and fury, signifying nothing ...*"

"Are you all right, Mr Shakespeare?" Toby asked. He was sure he had heard those words being spoken by Macbeth in the play, and that wasn't a good sign – things hadn't turned out well for the Scottish King. "Is there anything I can do?"

"Yes, you can tell me how I got to the point where I paid a band of thieves to put a rival play-house out of business," said Will. "It *was* wrong. No offence, Toby."

"None taken," Toby said. "You were desperate, and I know what that's like. I didn't want to become a pick-pocket myself, but the Plague carried off my parents and left me on my own. So it was either work for Moll Cut-Purse or starve to death."

"Now I feel even more guilty," said Will. "You had a really hard choice to make, but I didn't. I could just give up my life here and go back to Stratford, where I'm from. I should do it for my wife, anyway. Things haven't been all that easy for her."

Will explained that he had come to London twenty years ago to make his name as an actor and writer. But his wife Anne had stayed in Stratford, so they hadn't seen much of each other – Will had only been able to make short trips home. He had made enough money to buy a big house in Stratford, yet he was hardly ever there. That meant Anne had to keep everything going by herself.

"I also have two grown-up daughters," said Will. He smiled, although Toby could see his eyes were sad. "We had a son, too," Will added. "But he died when he was about your age. So you and I both know what it is to lose the people we love."

They sat in a brooding silence for a while,

thinking about that.

There was a big, three-masted ship on the river, and as Toby watched, some sailors started raising the anchor. Others clambered up the rigging, setting the sails to catch the breeze.

"What are you going to do, then?" Toby asked at last, and Will shrugged.

"Give up, I

suppose," he said. "The only thing that's stopped me admitting defeat before now is that I want The Globe to survive whether I'm around or not – many people depend on it for a living. Besides, it's where I've spent most of my working life, and I'd hate to see everything we've built up vanish and be forgotten. But Ned Alleyn is right. We need a new hit play – and I'm getting nowhere with it."

Toby didn't like the idea of The Globe going bust either. He had spent a lot of time there over the last couple of weeks, watching and listening. He had come to see how everybody worked together to make Will's wonderful plays come to life on the stage. Now Toby knew he would give anything to work at The Globe as well, and live an honest life, of course. He didn't want to be a pick-pocket any more, and he certainly didn't want to be a beggar. Maybe he could help Will with a few suggestions ... His eyes strayed back to the sailors, busy with their tasks.

"You should write a play about a voyage," he said, nodding at the ship in the river. "That's the kind of new thing everybody is interested in. I've just read this amazing book about some people who were shipwrecked and had to live on an island."

"That sounds interesting," Will said. "What's the title of the book?"

"*A Discovery of the Bermudas*," said Toby. "I'll lend it to you if you like."

"That would be good." Will fell silent and seemed to be thinking. "I'd need a plot," he said after a while. "Something strong, a conflict with plenty of suspense."

"How about a struggle, like the one between you and Ned Alleyn?" Toby said. "He wants to take your place, conspires against you, and you defeat him with a secret plan."

"I like it!" said Will, sitting up. Then he slumped down again. "But it doesn't have any magic in it, does it? We need a play that King James will like, and he's obsessed with magic. I thought he would love *Macbeth* – after all, he was King of Scotland before he became King of England as well. But he complained because there was no magic in the first version. So I had to re-write it and put in all that weird stuff with the witches. Just how am I going to get magic into a play set on a desert island?"

"Simple!" Toby said. "You could make one of the characters a magician."

Will turned to look at him, and a smile spread slowly across his face. "Has anyone ever told you what a very clever boy you are, young Master Toby Cuffe? That is *such* a good idea – especially if it's a magician using his powers to right a wrong."

"Sounds great," Toby said,

smiling back at him. "I would pay to see it. If I had any money."

Just then there was a flash of lightning and a distant rumble of thunder. The wind grew stronger, and Toby could hear the captain of the ship calling to his men.

"Come on, Toby!" Will said, jumping up. "I have a play to write!"

They got back to The Globe just before the rain began to fall.

SCENE EIGHT

I'll Drown My Book

Will shut himself in his room at The Globe and didn't come out for a month, and Heminges made sure he wasn't disturbed. In fact, the only person Will spoke to was Toby, who brought him his meals. A couple of times Will asked for Toby's help in sorting out something about one of the characters in the play, or a particularly tricky part of the plot. Toby said what he thought, and Will scribbled it all down.

Then one afternoon Will announced that the play was finished, and he called a meeting of the sharers. They met in the same room as usual, and Will gave them a rough outline. Toby listened, enchanted, as Will talked.

The play was about a ship wrecked on an island, a conflict between a magician and the brother who had stolen his Dukedom. But Will's imagination had come up with so much more.

"It sounds great, Will," Phillips said. "Up to date, plenty of audience appeal …"

"We'll need to talk about casting," said Condell. "What did you have in mind?"

"Nobody could play the villain better than Burbage," said Will, and Burbage grinned. "And, Armin, I've written a great part for you." Armin nodded, as if to say he expected nothing less. "But," Will said, "*I* will be playing Prospero, the main character."

"Are you sure, Will?" Heminges said. "You haven't done any acting for years."

"I'm absolutely certain," said Will. "I'd also like to offer a small part to someone who has been a great help to me. How would you like to be a player, Toby?"

"What, me?" Toby squeaked, surprised. Then he smiled. "I would love it."

"Good, that's settled then," said Will. "Right, my friends, let's get to work."

"What's the title, Will?" Heminges asked. "We'll need it for the playbills."

"Titles can be difficult," said Will. "But simple is always best, I think. Let's call it *The Tempest*. That's a fancy word for a storm, if any of you were wondering."

Thus began the busiest two weeks yet of Toby's life.

Heminges had the play copied so the players could learn their lines. They all read the whole play of course, but they also each had a roll of paper with just their own lines

written on it, along with their "cues" – the last line of what came before they had to speak. At first Toby was worried he wouldn't be able to remember his lines, but he didn't have too many to learn. He was playing Ariel, a magical spirit who did Prospero's bidding.

"Have you worked it out yet, Toby?" Will said one day during rehearsal. "Prospero couldn't do any of what he wants without Ariel's help ... I based him on you."

"Aw, thanks," Toby murmured, blushing.

"I didn't do all that much, really."

They rehearsed every morning, before the play-house opened for the afternoon show. Everyone was measured for their costumes, which were fantastic. There was a lot of music in the play, so that had to be written and practised by the company's musicians. Will directed everything, and sometimes it seemed to be going well, while at other times it seemed like a disaster. They forgot their lines, they bumped into each other, they argued. But Toby could see it was gradually coming together.

Heminges had playbills made, and had them posted all over the city in the week before opening night.

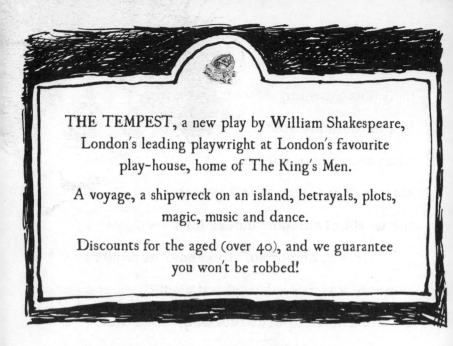

THE TEMPEST, a new play by William Shakespeare, London's leading playwright at London's favourite play-house, home of The King's Men.

A voyage, a shipwreck on an island, betrayals, plots, magic, music and dance.

Discounts for the aged (over 40), and we guarantee you won't be robbed!

Will had in fact sent Toby to Moll with an offer – free entry to *The Tempest* for her and her boys, so long as she made sure that absolutely no thieving happened.

"That Will Shakespeare drives a hard bargain." Moll sighed, but she was smiling. "Oh, go on, then. Tell him to throw in a mug

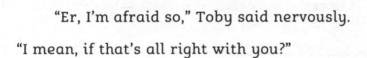

of beer each and
he'll have nothing
to worry about. And
what about you, young
Master Cuffe? Have I lost you to
the world of the play-house for ever?"

"Er, I'm afraid so," Toby said nervously.
"I mean, if that's all right with you?"

"Well, let's put it this way," she said. "I
have a feeling you'll make a better player than
you ever would a thief. You'd back me up on
that, wouldn't you, Jack?"

"I don't really know," Jack said, smiling
wickedly. "He's certainly a pretty useless thief,
but will he be a good player? I suppose we'll
just have to wait and see."

Toby laughed with them, but by the time he got back to the play-house he felt more nervous than ever. He was surprised to find out that Will was worried too.

"Of course I am!" said Will. "It doesn't matter how many plays I've written, or how many parts I've acted, it could all go horribly wrong the next time. The audience might hate the play, or I might act badly. You just have to be brave and do your best."

At last the big day arrived. Toby peered out from behind the stage as the play-house

slowly began to fill. There was a buzz of excitement in the audience, and in the players as well. Some laughed as they got changed, but some sat silently, pale-faced and muttering their lines to themselves. Toby felt as if a thousand giant butterflies were fluttering madly in his stomach, and he couldn't stop his hands shaking.

Then the play began.

The first scene was the shipwreck, and Toby didn't appear until the second scene. He felt sick as he waited to go onstage, but then he heard his cue and walked out to face Will, or Prospero as he was now. Toby opened his mouth to speak his lines, and for a second his mind went blank. Then they came to him.

"*All hail, great master! Grave sir, hail ...*"
Will's words flowed from Toby's mouth, and
suddenly he wasn't Toby any more, he was a
spirit called Ariel.

Will smiled and nodded,
and the scene was over almost
before Toby realised. He watched
the next scene, peering out from
behind the stage, and saw that the audience
was gripped. There was laughter as the play
unfolded, scene by scene, and booing for the
villains. But often the play-house was silent,
everyone utterly focused on the story.

Some things went wrong. Some of the
players forgot a line or two, but the others
kept going and the audience didn't seem to
notice. Towards the end of the play everything
seemed to speed up, scenes moving quickly,
the plot coming together. Toby was entranced
by the whole experience, whether he was on

stage or not. He found a couple of Prospero's speeches particularly moving, even sad.

Prospero talked about the magical things he had made happen on the island, and said they were almost over now. *"These our actors were all spirits, and are melted into thin air ... The great globe itself shall dissolve, and leave not a rack behind ..."*

Then, a little further on, Prospero announced that he would throw away his book of spells and give up magic for ever. "*I'll break my staff and I'll drown my book ...*" he declared.

Then it was over, and the audience was clapping and cheering wildly. Will led the players out on stage to take a bow with Toby

beside him. Toby saw Moll and Jack, grinning and waving their mugs of beer at him. He looked up at the galleries, and there was Sir Edmund Tilney grinning and clapping too.

Toby turned to Will. "All that stuff about drowning your book," he said. "You're not really going to give all this up, are you?"

Will looked at him and smiled. But he didn't say a word.

EPILOGUE

The Tempest proved to be a hit. It was a runaway success, and played to packed houses every day for weeks.

After Sir Edmund Tilney's recommendation, the play was put on at the Palace of Whitehall for the King, his family, and the entire royal court.

"Quite one of the most enjoyable plays I've seen in a long time, Master Shakespeare," King James said in his soft Scottish accent. "In fact, I'd say it was rather ... magical."

"Life is a joy, isn't it, Toby?" said Will later. "One day you're a common thief, then a few weeks later you're acting in a play for King James himself. Your rise isn't going to end here, either. I'm sure you have a great future ahead of you."

Things did go well for Toby. The sharers offered him a permanent job at The Globe. The days flew past in rehearsals and performances and all the work that had to be done at the play-house. They were very busy. There were more performances at the Palace, and extra performances

at The Globe itself. The other play-houses –
and Ned Alleyn – looked on enviously at the
terrific success of The King's Men.

All the young playwrights now wanted
to work for The Globe, so Will was able to do
what Heminges had said. He came up with
plots, and other writers did most of the hard
work.

"I don't want to give up writing for ever, I enjoy it too much for that," Will said to Toby. "But it's good not to be under pressure to deliver. I can spend more time at home in Stratford. I'm looking forward to a long life of doing very little."

But it was not to be. In 1616, five years after the first performance of *The Tempest*, Will was taken ill at a party for his birthday, and he died. The remaining sharers closed The Globe for a week so everyone could go to Will's funeral in Stratford. For Toby it was almost like losing his parents all over again, and he felt very glum for a while. Then he realised that Will would have wanted him to be happy, and he cheered up.

More time passed, and Toby grew to be a young man. He had acted many parts, including some of the women's roles in Will's plays, and those by other writers. He decided at last that he didn't want to act so much, and took over more of the running of The Globe. That suited him very well, and the sharers too. Before long they made Toby a sharer as well, and as he was so good at business, he became rather wealthy. Certainly prosperous enough to marry Sarah, a lovely girl he met one evening at The Globe.

One day in 1623, twelve years after the first performance of *The Tempest*, Heminges and Condell came to see Toby in his room at The Globe – the same room where he had first

met Will. Heminges handed Toby a large book
bound in brown leather.

"There you are, Toby – Will's plays, all
printed in one volume," Heminges said. "That's
the first copy, hot off the printing press. It
looks good, doesn't it?"

"Yes, it does. Will would have been very proud of it," said Toby. "How many copies have they printed? I hope we can make a profit for Anne and Will's daughters."

"Oh, no need to worry about that," said Condell. "They'll sell like hot cakes. But this copy is for you, Toby. Will would have wanted you to have one."

Toby took the book home and showed it to Sarah. They lived together in a small house in a quiet part of the city, and Sarah was expecting their first baby.

"How about calling the baby Will if it's a boy?" Toby said.

Somehow it just seemed the right thing to do.

ACT II

Funne Activities for
Boyes & Girls

SCENE ONE

_____

The Busy Streets of London

Stop the thief!

Hear ye, hear ye!

Squeeeeaaak!

In Shakespeare's time, the streets of London were dangerous, smelly, crowded and full of life. You might see a dancing bear, a woman selling pies or gangs of rats on the prowl. You might smell the perfume of rich ladies and gentlemen, or perhaps it would be swamped by the stink of chamber pots being emptied out of the windows into the street. You'd have to watch out for nippers, dippers and all the other criminals ducking and diving among the crowds.

Turn the page for a street scene with lots to spot ...

Rats

A fiddler

A beggar

Someone in the stocks

A dog stealing its dinner

A man emptying a chamber pot

A pick-pocket ... or two
A monk
A knife fight
A seller of books
A dancing bear
A town crier

SCENE TWO

All the World's a Stage

"All the world's a stage,
And all the men and women merely
players ..."

The Globe was a busy place. When plays
were put on, it would be full of people, rich
and poor. Rich people sat in the gallery and
poor people jostled for a place in the pit, the
ground in front of the stage. The crowd would
be noisy and would buy food and drink from

the sellers at the door. If they didn't enjoy the play, they might throw their food and drink at the stage! In other parts of the building, there were rooms where Will Shakespeare and the company worked on new plays, had meetings and stored their costumes, make-up and sets. When plays weren't taking place, The Globe might be used for other entertainments such as bear-baiting and dog-fighting.

Turn the page for a scene at The Globe with lots to spot ...

- A portrait of Queen Elizabeth I
- A man with a bear
- A 'flying' actor
- A canon, used for smoke and special effects
- A man with a trumpet to signal the start of the play
- A man playing a woman on stage

SCENE THREE

The Show Must Go On!

Turn the page to find the main cast members of *The Tempest*. Trace the figures onto thin card and draw your own costumes for each character.

- **Prospero** is a wizard. He would wear a cloak, but it might be a little tatty as he has been exiled for a long time.

- **Ariel** is a spirit. He would wear wispy fabric.

- **Caliban** is a monster. He would wear shaggy fur and rags.

Miranda is Prospero's daughter. She would wear a dress that is a bit ragged.

Ferdinand is a young nobleman. He would be smartly dressed.

Cut out your finished cast and glue each character onto a lolly stick or straw. Now you can stage *The Tempest*!

You can download a simple script and a model of The Globe to make at **www.barringtonstoke. co.uk/books/the-boy-and-the-globe**.

Toby Cuffe as

Ariel

William Shakespeare as

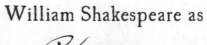

Richard Burbage as

Caliban

Henry Condell as

Ferdinand

Robert Armin as

Miranda

SCENE FOUR

Barbs with the Bard

When Shakespeare's characters are angry, they use some very colourful insults. Next time you fall out with one of your friends, try these insults out for size ...

Thou art like a toad; ugly and venomous.

from *As You Like It*

Thou crusty batch of nature!

from *Troilus and Cressida*

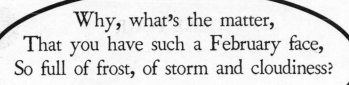

Why, what's the matter,
That you have such a February face,
So full of frost, of storm and cloudiness?

From *Much Ado About Nothing*

Mountain goat!

from *Henry V*

A pox o' your
throat, you bawling,
blasphemous,
incharitable dog!

From *The Tempest*

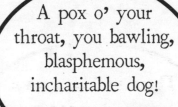

You eel-skin,
you dried
neat's-tongue!

**from *Henry IV
Part 1***

IF YOU ENJOYED
the Boy and the Globe
YOU MIGHT LIKE ...

Robyn and her Merry Men live deep in the forest. They wear brown (not green), but they do like to rob from the rich to give to the poor, foil dastardly knights, and go on quests ...

This book was written by (Sir) Philip Ardagh, who takes being funny very seriously indeed. Writing this book was no laughing matter (except for the funny parts).

TWANG! DUCK!

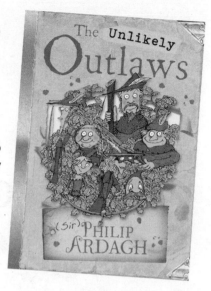

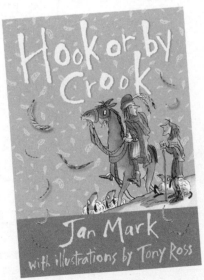

The Abbott of Canterbury is for the chop. Mean King John has set him three puzzles. If the Abbott cannot answer, he'll lose his head.

Robin Hood is about to lose his dinner. He's top outlaw in the forest. But his new career is far from plain sailing!

With foul facts, queasy quizzes and pestilent puzzles, *Hook or by Crook* is Middle Ages mayhem!

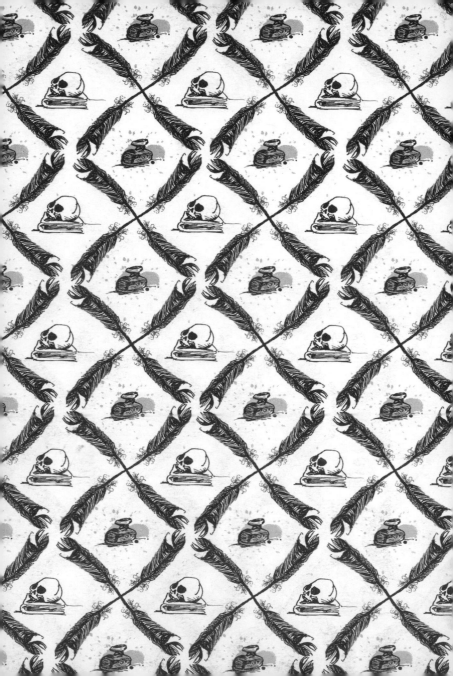